Renewable Energy

a short story about second chances

By Beyr Reyes

Renewable Energy:
A Short Story About Second Chances
Beyr Reyes
Copyright @ 2016 ShadeTree Publishing, LLC
Print ISBN: 978-1-937331-84-9
e-Book ISBN: 978-1-937331-85-6
Cover art by Nejron Photo

Visit our Web site at www.ShadeTreePublishing.com.

He has made known to us his secret plan, which by his own will, he designed beforehand in connection with his son and will put into effect when the time is ripe.

Ephesians 1:9–10 CJB (paraphrased)

The Master Plan

Gabor secretly watched as Agent Kane penned another entry into his journal. He noted how the writer appeared distressed—and understandably so, given the big event scheduled for later in the day.

Gabor, the commander's head courier and messenger, had been covertly observing Agent Kane for generations, so he knew his habits and hangouts, which he regularly reported to his leader.

Kane finally finished his composition and hid the book in its usual spot behind a hand-carved chest. Gabor was careful to remain concealed as Kane shuffled about the room, readying himself for an urgent departure. Kane's movements suggested that he sensed a presence in the room. He blew right past the cloaked Gabor on his way out the door.

Gabor wasted no time getting down to work. He was on a special assignment to deliver Kane's journal to the commander.

He slipped his hand behind the chest and found the familiar-feeling book. It was soft to the touch, owing to the well-worn leather binding. Gabor rolled the journal from hand to hand until it fell open. Although not the first time he had peered into Kane's written thoughts, it was definitely the most important. Today started the finale of the master plan. Gabor wondered whether Kane would survive the process.

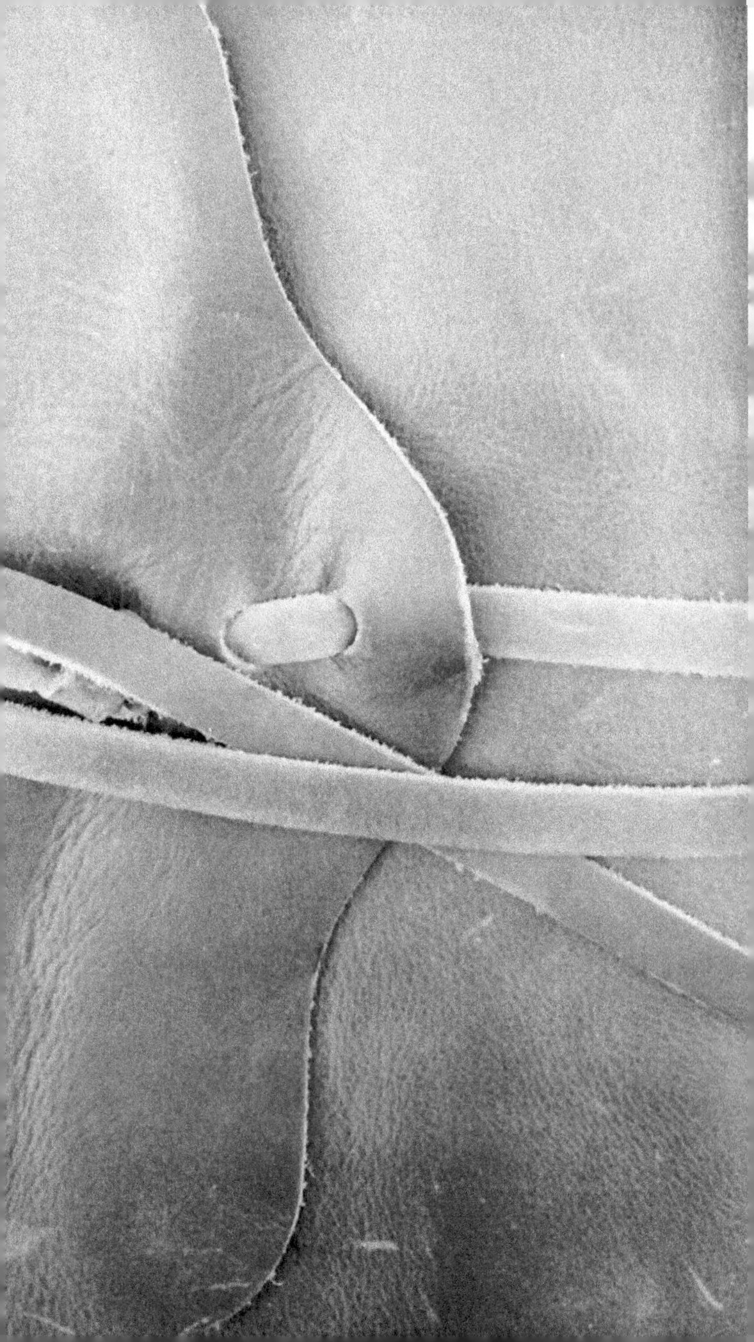

Entry 03-45.98.0
in the beginning

My name is Agent Kane, and I am a watcher in Commander Abaddon's forces on Planet Ge. Because this is my first journal, I'll begin by telling how everything started and how I got here.

Long ago, my current leader, Commander Abaddon, served in a great kingdom and was second in command only to Supreme Leader Sook. Abaddon carried Sook's signet and had full freedom to operate in his authority. He was also Sook's trusted advisor and was privy to all of Sook's ambitions and strategies. That is, until the Ge Initiative...

Sook announced an unexpected—and yet obviously planned—trip to the small planet Ge in the Lecha star system. When they arrived on the surface, Sook began planting something mysterious and offered no explanations. Despite constant interrogation, Abaddon kept getting the same cryptic response from Sook, "It is good." Abaddon quickly realized that he had been left out of the need-to-know loop right from the start, and Sook was not going to provide any clarity.

Eventually, the plantings grew and produced terrestrial beings who not only could communicate, but also reproduce after their kind. Sook never missed a moment to dote on his new creation (nicknamed "the dwellers"), and he gave them a strict commandment to multiply, which they aptly did. What was a growing adoration for Sook became a burgeoning point of contention for Abaddon.

Sook never explained his intentions for the new Ge dwellers, but he made it clear that they were off-limits to Abaddon. This withholding only made the control of Ge more desirable for Abaddon. This was the one part of Sook's kingdom that was now unauthorized for him, and it incited an insatiable coveting of power that he didn't try to hide.

Abaddon finally convinced his buddies to defect from Sook's command with him. Shortly after, Sook abandoned Abaddon and his followers on Ge, declaring that if Abaddon wanted control of Ge so much, then he could rule over it—_and only it._

When everything went down, I, too, found myself on the scorned and forsaken side of Sook, so I pledged my allegiance to Commander Abaddon.

It was the beginning of the dwellers and the visitors living together on Ge, and the beginning of the end.

Entry 03-66.98.5
after the fallout

When Commander Abaddon first found me, I was a real mess. I had just been "released" from Sook's services.

My coworker and I had each prepared a special assignment as requested by Sook. Mine was on Ge's flora, and his was on the fauna.

It took me a long time to prepare my report because I had to wait for the right season and pollination phase. It was a lot of vigilant watching and waiting. Something I was good at.

Despite all my effort, and for some unknown reason, Sook hated my report and rejected me. I couldn't understand why, and my requests for an explanation were answered with a dismissal. Before I could leave, Sook cursed me with a burned mark across my face so that everyone would know and recognize me. I can still feel the sting today...and the scar hurts sometimes, too.

Commander Abaddon was the first to find me after I wandered into the wilderness. It was almost like he was there, ready to catch me when Sook threw me away. He took in this forsaken outcast and gave me another life.

Now I am one of the watchers in Commander Abaddon's army. Our job is to monitor the actions of the dwellers and report our findings to him. (Abaddon is obsessed with the dwellers. His fixation only slightly outweighs his hatred for them.)

No one, including Abaddon, really understands why Sook planted the dwellers on Ge and what exactly he put in them. It's almost like he placed a piece of himself in them, which makes Abaddon despise them even more. This "thing" in the dwellers is a sort of energy that can be seen by the visitors, but not by the other dwellers. (I should also mention that visitors are invisible to dwellers unless they choose to reveal themselves. It's a handy ability for most watchers.)

Sook continues to visit the dwellers on occasion. He also sends his leaders to assist them. Most of the time, the helpers operate incognito and are unbeknownst by the dwellers. Visitors, though, can see this activity surrounding the dwellers, and subsequently they put these special ones on a watch list.

Abaddon constantly tries to understand what the dwellers actually are and why Sook is so interested in them. As such, the job of a watcher is revered, and competition for the positions is intense.

There are two basic types of a watcher: those who watch important dwellers, and those who watch entire families and their offspring down through the generations. Sometimes really important dwellers may have multiple watchers. Those who watch families are able to track heritable weaknesses that can be predicted and exploited in later generations. I've heard stories about how some weaknesses, like substance abuse and emotional imbalance, spread like a winding vine though the dwellers' lineage. The instigators (other visitors who work hand in hand with the watchers) have learned how to propagate and direct this vine by covertly manipulating events in the dwellers' lives. We watchers and instigators have made a game of it, and we even make wagers on the outcomes.

As for me, I didn't want to be a family watcher, because I can't keep a family myself, and watching other families only disgusts me. So instead, I generally take on high-profile, individual dwellers.

I spend my time observing Sook's most beloved pets, and I must say, I do a great job. On my best days, Commander Abaddon acknowledges me—in his own special way, of course—and sometimes I come away with no new bruises.

We watchers have been successful so far. Our first assignments revolved around the initial shock wave of the fallout, but now we wait for the dust to settle while Abaddon contemplates his next steps.

Entry 09-95.91.9
crossing the line

Monitoring the reproduction process of dwellers is not my idea of the perfect assignment. Unlike the visitors, the dwellers reproduce though a specific type of physical interaction, after an acceptable social pairing (which they call "marriage"), and they tend to stick with a single mate for a lifetime. (Not sure how it would feel to have someone by my side for all my life. I'm a loner by necessity.)

Because we noticed that dwellers could crossbreed amongst themselves,

Abaddon came up with the crazy plan to try crossing the lineage of dwellers with visitors.

Personally...I don't get it. Why is Abaddon so obsessed with the dwellers? Is it only because he hates them, or is there something else?

Perhaps Abaddon sees himself in the dwellers. Many times, the flaws that strike us in others are actually the ones that are most prevalent in ourselves, and others are simply a mirror reflecting our own image. If so, then maybe he wants to extinguish the dwellers so that he doesn't have to see his own selfishness and pride.

Or perhaps, when Abaddon looks at the dwellers, he sees how frail and pitiful they are, and yet he realizes that Sook chose them over him. It doesn't take a genius to work out those implications.

For someone who hates another so much, it sure is strange how Abaddon tries to live like the dwellers. For example, when he told us about this latest plan, he was attempting to eat their food. He does this sort of thing all the time.

That day, like many others, he sat at his royal table and scarfed down as much food as he could. It didn't take long for the binged substances to come hurling back out and all over everything in their path. Like it was no consequence to him, he called in the royal dogs to eat up the spewed feast and started the process all over again. During one of his previous indulgences, he flew off in a rage, shoved me down in his vomit, and called me his disgusting mutt. He's always telling me that he sees me for what I am.

Speaking of mutts...

Abaddon eventually found a way to crossbreed visitors with dwellers. We named the offspring "nephilim."

Physically, they are bigger, like the visitors, but they have no abilities like them. What they possess in strength and brawn, they equally lack in intelligence. The nephilim are prone to strife and fighting and show little allegiance to Abaddon, or even Sook for that matter. They seek to set up their own kings to subdue the dwellers. (Obviously this was a surprising twist that Abaddon didn't account for.)

Abaddon is not the only one upset with the results of the nephilim experiment. Sook declared it an "energy contamination issue" and has vowed to correct it. When

Abaddon crossed the visitors and dwellers, he actually crossed a line. Now, all I can do is wait it out and hope I'm on the right side.

Entry 11-61.94.1
the great liquidation

It didn't take long for Sook to put his decontamination plan into action. Immediately, the watchers noted increased interest and activity around one particular dweller. That's when I was summoned by Abaddon.

When I arrived at his war-planning chamber, located in a discreet location on Ge, Abaddon tossed me a detailed report from another watcher. It contained information on my new assignment—

a special dweller who was receiving so much of Sook's attention.

Abaddon bragged on the report and how much he appreciated the author of it while shooting barbs of sarcasm toward me with his eyes. Then he told me to go see what a real "beloved dweller" looked like. I felt the implications of what he was saying, and the reminder of a certain reporting incident in my past. Nevertheless, I swallowed my disdain and pretended not to notice. At this point, my options are limited. I have to make the best of my situation. Abaddon knows my predicament and continually reminds me of how he "allows" me to continue in his service. That he sees me for what I'm worth.

During my observations of this so-called beloved dweller, I quickly ascertained that he really wasn't all that special. Apparently he had been given a specific task from Sook, because he was always hard at work building something. It took me a while to figure out that he was constructing a huge transport ship.

I reported all my findings to Abaddon, who surmised that Sook must be preparing to take all his dwellers and run. He instructed me to hide aboard the ship and gather more intel.

Even as I write this now, I am a stowaway, carefully concealed in the shadows on the great vessel. I sit here in absolute horror of what I am witnessing. Instead of thousands of dwellers onboard, there are only a handful. The rest are locked outside the ship and drowning in a boundless flood.

Sook never intended to collect his cherished dwellers...he meant to kill them all. His plan was liquidation. To reboot, restart, and return to ground-state energy. Sook is turning over a new leaf with his plantings.

Entry 14-12.97.1
increasing polarity

Since the Great Flood, the handful of dwellers who survived didn't waste any time reproducing. The tragedy of the loss, along with a renewed appreciation of life, strengthened their resolve and unity.

Abaddon cancelled the nephilim project and cut his losses, as well. All the generations-long information gathering and planning he had completed was decimated in the flood, too.

At first, things moved slowly while the dweller population replenished itself. Because of the small number of dwellers, there weren't enough assignments to go around for all the watchers, so I had plenty of time to mull over the events of the recent annihilation. I still can't reconcile how Sook could claim to love something so much and yet turn around and destroy it. I'm in total denial of how one being could do that to another.

Eventually the dwellers grew into a mighty unit that worked with one mind and one accord. As they labored together, their efforts proved to be synergistic. In addition, they also gradually became aware of the energy within themselves. It didn't take long for the dwellers to add one plus one and decide to build a massive structure, which somehow coalesced their internal energy and resulted in a kind of power cell. Honestly, none of us watchers understood what was really going on, and the dwellers obviously had no idea of the potentially devastating consequences of their actions. However, we all knew it must have been really bad when Sook stepped in to demolish the towering structure and then scatter the dwellers across the surface of Ge. Afterward, he even caused them to all speak different languages so the various groups couldn't communicate with each other any longer. Once again, Sook the destroyer.

Abaddon saw how Sook had broken the unity of the dwellers, and he decided to use the tactic for himself. He devised a long-term plan that would run in the background of his other campaigns. He vowed to polarize Sook's dwellers and sway their allegiance.

Abaddon's divide-and-conquer approach was successful right from the start. He isolated leaders with the stresses of responsibility and accountability. He unraveled marriages with something called divorce. He even introduced "dwellerism," which is the promotion of self over all other things. Many dwellers now live their lives as if they are the single most important thing on the planet and everything else exists to serve their needs. Their blatant self-regard alienates them from others.

Abaddon also established something called "religion," whereby dwellers offer their worship and allegiance to fictitious "gods" and revoke their allegiance to Sook. The dwellers divide themselves into different sects and bicker over the doctrine and politics inherent to each one.

Abaddon introduced new technology to the dwellers, making it possible for them to interact socially without being in physical proximity to one another. Not only is this decreasing good reproductive pairing, but also the dwellers are gradually losing their sense of family and community. Many dwellers are using this technology and substituting the acquisition of knowledge for relationships.

Most of Abaddon's initiatives work with little input from his instigators; however, they continue to have their fun by masquerading as messengers from Sook and tricking the dwellers. They deliver fictitious messages that lead the dwellers off of Sook's path and purpose for them. They love to give opposing "messages from Sook" to different dwellers and then watch them argue over who is correct and who knows more, when in fact, they both are wrong, or, in the really funny cases, they are both right.

Sook doesn't seem to like Abaddon's handiwork of dissention

and division. He responded by assembling a special task force of dwellers called the Sookotes, who were instructed to live apart from the other dwellers and thus away from their influences.

None of us watchers understand how the Sookotes were chosen or what makes them special. For example, are they special because they are Sookotes, or are they Sookotes because they are special? Very confusing! Nevertheless, they soon became envied among the dwellers because they were publicly acknowledged as Sook's chosen group. It doesn't help that Sook continually favors them and affords them special protection. It makes other dwellers feel inadequate and unwanted.

Abaddon does everything he can to propagate ill will toward the Sookotes. He also tries to destroy them and hinder anything they set out to accomplish. He plays on the resentment and jealousy the other dwellers have toward the Sookotes and uses it to further propagate his goals of polarization.

Abaddon's efforts are extremely successful. Not only is there a clear division of the visitors between him and Sook, but also the plantlings are being separated into the wheat and tares. As for me, I'm not sure where I belong.

Entry 17-07.85.0
quest for soular energy

So, the dwellers have this sort of energy in them that we call soular energy. As I've explained before, visitors can see this energy emanating from the dwellers, but other dwellers cannot.

I've been told that the planet Ge is like a huge dry-cell battery that can store energy. It has two poles and three distinct layers. The inner core is the cathode and the outer shell is the anode, and the mantle is in between. (And that's the extent of my scientific knowledge about it, so that's all I'll say about the matter.)

The visitors quickly noticed that when dwellers "died," their soular energy separated from their physical body and was transferred to a collection-like point in the belly of the planet. Because the visitors could see this energy accumulation, they named the whereabouts Sheol.

After the Great Flood, the intensity of Sheol grew exponentially, and the flash really got Abaddon's attention. He reasoned that Sook had created the dwellers as a means of replicating energy that could be stored in the planet until he was ready to harvest it. Not willing to be outdone, Abaddon set out to claim the soular energy for himself and become more powerful than Sook...his most ambitious plan yet.

Abaddon turned his initial focus onto the live dwellers. He enlisted the help of some dweller leaders and scientists, promising them that they could be planet leaders if they did his bidding. They were all too eager, and they started with the Sookotes, whom they abducted by whole communities at once.

The scientists did all sorts of probing experiments, trying to find the physical location of the energy within the body. Then they unabashedly began dissecting the dwellers. All to no avail. Their last resort was to "release" the energy from the living dwellers by using various techniques. Many dwellers were burned alive in incinerators, sometimes a hundred at once. I was sure the putrid smell would have roused the scientists out of their madness and pursuit for power, but alas, it did not. Other scientists used acids and detergents to dissolve the dwellers, and hopefully their energy, so that it could be extracted chemically.

When all of the experiments on the live dwellers didn't bear fruit, Abaddon turned his attention to the energy stored in Sheol. Twice he had been a witness to architectural structures that were able to hold and focus soular energy. The first had been the tower the dwellers had built when they were united. The second was in a technologically advanced city (made so thanks to input by the visitors) located on an island in one of Ge's vast oceans. Both construction projects had similar results. In the first incident, Sook destroyed the tower and scattered the dwellers, and in the second incident, he sank the entire island and its inhabitants.

Abaddon then decided to attempt to build a massive structure for himself. His advisors helped him to develop giant pyramids that would act as energy funnels to syphon the energy out of Sheol. To his dismay, the pyramids didn't work, because dweller kings used them as royal burial chambers, thus disrupting the energy flow. (The kings wanted to become gods and thought this burial technique would be a surefire way to make it happen.)

Abaddon was also working on an alternate plan, using the pyramids as molds for giant terrariums to "grow" his own dwellers. (This is why he preferred to position the structures in desert regions with high silica levels.) I never heard anything more about this plan, so perhaps he abandoned it.

As Abaddon was building the pyramids, and using dweller labor to accomplish it, he stumbled onto the answer he had been searching for. It started out by Abaddon pretending to be one of the fictitious gods he had previously created in order to persuade the dwellers to build the structures, even at the cost of their own lives. He really got into character and began to dress the part, with jewels and precious metals adorning his entire body. When the laborers needed motivation to work harder, Abaddon would reveal himself to the dwellers. He conjured a body that was similar to the dwellers' bodies, but was enhanced by beauty, vigor, strength, and an abundance of majesty. His appearance commanded respect, and the dwellers freely gave it.

Abaddon fell bewitched by his own appearance. He maintained this new facade even in his private abode, and was quick to point out anything he perceived to be ugliness. More than once I caught his sneers when he looked at the scar across my face.

It didn't take long for the dwellers to turn their affections toward Abaddon. He strengthened the rapport by answering their prayers for water and plentiful crops (an easy thing to manipulate for visitors).

The dwellers' affections soon transformed into worship, which had an unexpected effect on Abaddon—it caused him to grow in power. This phenomenon had something to do with the dwellers' energy. When they worshiped Abaddon, it was as if they were voluntarily relinquishing their own energy to him, and thus he became stronger. This was the first time he was ever successful at obtaining soular energy.

The more energy Abaddon collects, the more powerful he becomes, and the more powerful he becomes, the more influence he has over the dwellers and thus the more energy he is able to collect. A no-miss win.

Abaddon's primary plan thus shifted toward gaining dweller worshipers. With his eye also on the bounty of the raw soular energy waiting for him in Sheol, he intensified investigations on how to extract it. Meanwhile, he set up his kingdom near Sheol and built a secure container to hold his soon-to-be-gained energy booty. He is so proud of this furnace-like unit that he keeps the keys to it framed on his wall.

Every day that Abaddon gains more worshiper energy, his appetite becomes even more insatiable, and he morphs into a more sinister being. He is bent on consuming all the soular energy that ever existed on Ge—no matter the cost.

Entry 20-31.77.4
weapons of mass destruction

As soon as Abaddon learned that he grows more powerful when dwellers worship him, he came up with a twofold plan:

1) Convert as many dwellers as possible to his kingdom, by romancing the indifferent and frustrating other dwellers and turning them against Sook.

2) Kill or disable any dwellers who remain allegiant to Sook.

Abaddon often crows about his plan, because it offers him a chance to grow stronger than Sook while at the same time, steal Sook's beloved creation and hurt him. He especially targets the Sookotes and the youth—Sook's favorite dwellers.

The weapons that Abaddon uses are not swords, guns, or other artillery. They are far more sinister and include things like doubt, stress, illness, poverty, unforgiveness, and pride. These are weapons that the dwellers don't see coming and certainly don't understand how to defeat. Abaddon is wreaking havoc on Ge, both on the dwellers and on the planet itself.

Dwellers were already prone to want to subdue one another, so Abaddon uses things like government corruption, philosophical doctrine, and the love of money to create anarchy and dissention. It does not take long for sects to fight among one other, especially in the name of their own pet causes.

Wars are used to kill dwellers with loyal and patriotic hearts for Sook and to incite hate and lust in others, with the goal of readying them for Abaddon's appeal.

Societal pruning is used to swing the odds in Abaddon's favor.

Abaddon aims for the degradation of societies and uses things like drugs, illicit sex, prejudice, and social violence. He especially targets the younger dwellers to taint them at an earlier age, giving him more time to romance them. He is always joking about "making the dirt-beings dirty," and he developed another devious plan to sow corruption.

Abaddon's instigators use the watchers' notes to identify weaknesses and tendencies in the dwellers' lives and in their generational lineage. Then they use that information to arrange proper interventions to entrap the dwellers in addictions and depravity. One technique involves using signs that are flashed in front of a dweller's eyes at unsuspecting times. As an example, for the dwellers who deal with sexual perversion, the instigators flash explicit and erotic images before them. Those dwellers dealing with self-esteem issues receive snapshot images of themselves in the midst of prior failures, and those struggling with depression receive images provoking sadness, grief, and despair. Drug addicts get images of drugs, food addicts get images of food, and so on...

The instigators are careful to do their work undetected and remain invisible at all times. They allow the images to be seen for only a fraction of a moment—just long enough to subliminally jump-start the dweller's thinking in a certain area.

Sometimes I feel sorry for the dwellers, because they can be going along on their happy way when one of the signs interjects disturbing thoughts, and they cannot explain why, where, or how. To them, the impulses seem to come out of the blue. Eventually, the dwellers self-destruct.

Dwellers aren't the only things being destroyed. As Abaddon's kingdom grows in Ge's belly, it creates instability and energy imbalances in the planet. Ge quakes, and vicious storms increase in alarming numbers with each passing season. Mountaintops explode and vomit the molten innards of the planet, devouring everything in their vicinity with fire. Increased internal energy results in higher surface temperatures, and thus melting in the polar regions.

By trying to switch the poles and the electromagnetic field of Ge, Abaddon hopes to reverse the circuit of the battery-like effect that holds the soular energy in Sheol. (He is still trying to figure out how to get to that energy.) His attempts further threaten the very existence of the planet.

Abaddon is capitalizing on the destruction of Ge and maximizing his efforts to kill the planet and eventually eradicate any possibility of life on its surface. He plans to live in its belly in his own kingdom once he attains enough energy to surpass Sook. By destroying all life on the surface, he also hopes to destroy the chances of Sook gaining any more energy.

I have spent many generations of dwellers witnessing Abaddon's atrocities. His weapons cause widespread death and massive destruction. Ge groans from the imbalance his kingdom imposes and the environmental devastation he induces. Sometimes I cheer him on, and other times, I want to restrain his next punch. I feel trapped between the oppressed and the oppressor.

I'm not sure how much more Ge can endure. Will Sook do anything to save the dwellers, or will he forsake us all again?

Entry 65-44.94.3
Sook's ace in the hole

Yesterday I was summoned again, the first time since before the Great Flood. Needless to say, I was a bit concerned...

When I arrived at Abaddon's war-planning chamber, a handful of other watchers were already seated around the large table. I was instructed to take a seat while another watcher materialized at the presentation post. I nearly missed my seat when about twenty other watchers simultaneously appeared around me, as well.

The presenter explained that he had received inside information about someone important from Sook's command who was en route to Ge.

Several other watchers then took turns explaining the events of the mysterious being's arrival. Some told about special messengers that Sook had sent in advance, and others claimed they saw a bright light in the sky on the night he came.

Turns out—the mysterious visitor is Sook's son, Zuan. Apparently he is here on a special mission and he brought with him a machine of some sort. None of the watchers had ever seen anything like it before, and they only frustrated Abaddon with their descriptions of it.

After what seemed like hours of speculation about Zuan and his puzzling machine, Abaddon finally turned his focus toward me. I could tell by the malicious, yet pleased look on his face that his request would be filled with both hatred and the sweetness of vengeance. I wasn't sure whether the sentiment was meant for Sook, for me, or for us both.

Abaddon laid out my next assignment, along with a long list of stipulations. In short, I am to watch Zuan closely, but I am forbidden from interacting with him or letting myself be seen.

I can't comprehend, though, why I am the only watcher assigned to such an important figure. All I know is that I must take this assignment seriously because my life depends on it.

Tomorrow I will set out to observe Zuan for the first time. There is a new player on the scene with some sort of power in his hand, and I'm going to nail down what it is.

Although my job is to gather as much information about Zuan and his machine, what Abaddon really wants to know is how to kill them both. Sook may be revealing his hand and his ace in the hole, but Abaddon is the one digging another type of hole— a grave, that is.

Entry 65-45.95.0
renewable energy

This morning I set out for my first observation of Zuan. I didn't know what to expect, but I presumed he would look like a cross between a warrior and a creature of nobility. My heart contained a bit of trepidation, and yet there was curious excitement, too. To say I was shocked when I saw him is an understatement.

Zuan's appearance is unassuming at best. Nothing like his father, who is often robed in special garments that accentuate his power. Instead, Zuan dresses in meek dweller attire and surrounds himself with throngs of other dwellers.

Despite my best efforts to conceal my presence, Zuan had no trouble discerning it and looked right through the crowd at me with his piercing green eyes. He then beckoned me to him. I was frozen in place with indecision, until something in his eyes melted my hesitation and my feet carried me in his direction.

All I could think about was how to explain this to Abaddon. An unfathomable punishment surely would await me. The closer I got to

Zuan, though, the further away the worries fled.

Once I arrived before him, Zuan looked me straight in the eye and said, "I see you." The same three words I had heard so often from Abaddon. Except this time I didn't feel threatened...I was convicted. Those three words set off a flurry of emotions inside me. Zuan stood there silently, as if he was waiting for me to land.

Desperate to change the topic, I got straight to the point and asked Zuan why he had come to Ge. Once again, he stood in silence as he continued to bandage a young dweller's arm. Even though his eyes were on his task, his gaze still penetrated my heart.

He took his silent time tending to the youngster, then he accepted her appreciation and kissed the top of her head before she ran off to play.

"Come sit with me for a while," he finally said and motioned toward a nearby bench.

Without any reluctance, he began to answer every question I had about him and the machine. At times, it seemed like he was answering them as they popped into my head instead of waiting for them to exit my mouth.

Zuan explained that all dwellers contain an energy that, in its most basic form, is not sufficient to withstand the energy present in Sook's kingdom. All the energy-containing beings in the kingdom must be on the same level as Sook's or his energy would destroy them when they were in his presence. Zuan reckoned it to the radiation on Ge. Radiation will not destroy other radiation, but it can destroy things of lower energy.

If the dwellers were ever to be able to live in Sook's kingdom, they would need to have their energy renewed. To address this issue, Zuan had brought with him an energy renewal machine.

Sensing I was not the scientific type, Zuan patiently explained the machine. Apparently, it is a sort of light therapy that "purifies" the dwellers' internal energy by raising it from its ground state to a high-energy state.

As the dwellers pass through the machine, they are marked across their foreheads with Sook's seal, to serve as a testimony to others and to indicate that they have been processed for kingdom transport. The idea of being "sealed" across the face by Sook didn't set too well with me for obvious reasons.

Zuan stepped around my apparent discomfort, however, and explained how Sook had originally planted the dwellers in hopes of populating his kingdom with them. Zuan was sent to Ge to initiate all the conversions and ready the dwellers for transport.

Needless to say, I was at a loss for words. The answers that Abaddon had sought for generations had just been given to me in a matter of moments. It was a lot to take in.

Zuan allowed me a few moments to digest this meat, before standing to indicate our conversation had concluded. Before departing, he shook my hand and invited me to come see the machine up close as soon as I could.

I'm not sure how much longer I sat on that bench, but a rustling in the bushes startled me from my trance. Not able to discern the source of the noise, I scrambled to leave the scene as fast as I could. I knew it was possible that another watcher had been watching me and could be on the way back to Abaddon. I convinced myself that it was what we watchers joke about: watcher paranoia an occupational hazard.

Now here I am vacillating, because I have the answers Abaddon wants (and it would behoove me to get to him before another watcher tattles on me), yet Zuan has the answers that I also want, and I long for the peace I felt when I was in his presence. I'm not sure about all this energy talk, but I certainly need to be renewed. I can't go on merely existing the way I have been. I've spent too many years unable to have a family and life like my fellow dwellers. Not to mention working for a boss who hates all dwellers, including me. I need to live again but am I worthy of a second chance? I've spent many generations betraying my own dweller kind.

Entry 65-58.95.3
the engine of change

After a long night of discussions with myself, I finally reasoned that it would be better to report to Abaddon with my current information. It was sufficient knowledge for him to plan his next move. Knowing the purpose of Zuan was enough, and the details of the machine were actually inconsequential.

After I delivered the information, Abaddon put his entire force on alert and explained his plans to execute Zuan within the fortnight.

With the stress of reporting gone, the invitation from Zuan wouldn't leave my mind. I resolved to visit him and the machine.

Zuan was waiting at the door for me when I arrived. He asked if I was ready. I took him to mean was I ready for the tour, even though I knew he intended something much more.

The machine is simpler than I had imagined. It looks like a tub filled with light instead of water. I watched as dwellers laid themselves on a slab and directed the operator to lower them into the tank. When they emerged, there was a noticeable difference in them. I had to squint, but I could make out a mark freshly written across their face.

Zuan asked whether I would like to take a closer look. As we ascended the platform stairs together, he told me a story.

"Two brothers were given an important assignment by the king. Each brother worked very hard on his task. Meanwhile, the king stopped in to check on them. One of the brothers felt that the king was favoring the other and allowed resentment to fill his heart and mind.

When reporting day came, the king accepted one of the brothers' reports and rejected the other from the jealous brother. Although the rejected report had everything it was supposed to have, also in it were accusations against the other brother. The king told the angry brother that his report was not a place to air his offenses and that he should have worked out his issues with his brother before submitting the report. The king instructed him to redo the report."

Zuan paused his story when we arrived beside the slab and asked if I had ever heard it. I understood at that very moment that Zuan really did *see* me. Yes, of course I knew the story, and all too well—I was the angry brother.

Then Zuan asked me how the story ends. I backed up from his question and accidentally brushed up against the slab, which felt like metallic destiny. The shock wave through my body created a flashback of the mis-chronicled event.

I saw the rejected report wrapped around a bloody rock as I threw it into a shallow hole. I had killed my own brother and buried the evidence.

The scene shifted like sand, and the next thing I saw was myself being questioned by Sook. I lied about everything, but Sook knew better. He sentenced me to walk the planet alone until I was willing to repent. He marked me with a seal to prevent others from killing me in the meantime.

All these images danced around my mind like a revolving carousel. Added to the chaos was every time that I had ever blamed Sook or cursed his name.

Zuan's slight touch on my right shoulder instantly plucked me out of the tumult. After giving me a minute to catch my breath, he launched into another story.

"There once was a son who forfeited his life with his father and sought another life far away. This new life was not all that he had anticipated, and he found himself in a very bad place. He finally decided that this new life was so much worse than returning home and facing his father for the actions he had taken and asking for forgiveness. Once he made his way back to the father's home, instead of facing an angry father, he was met with a father running toward him with open and forgiving arms."

Zuan told me how Sook loved me and spoke of me often. His powerful green eyes swirled with compassion. The news overwhelmed me and forced me to sit. Zuan then asked if I would like to be restored and renewed. I deeply contemplated his question. Was it even possible that I could be renewed? Would the commander really accept me back into the fold? My heart was stirred up with regret, embarrassment, turmoil, doubt, and everything in between. I felt too far gone and too embarrassed to face not only my actions, but also Sook himself.

I don't know whether the subsequent events were hallucinations brought about by the slab I was now sitting on, or whether they were real. All I know is that change is in the air. Even I can feel it now.

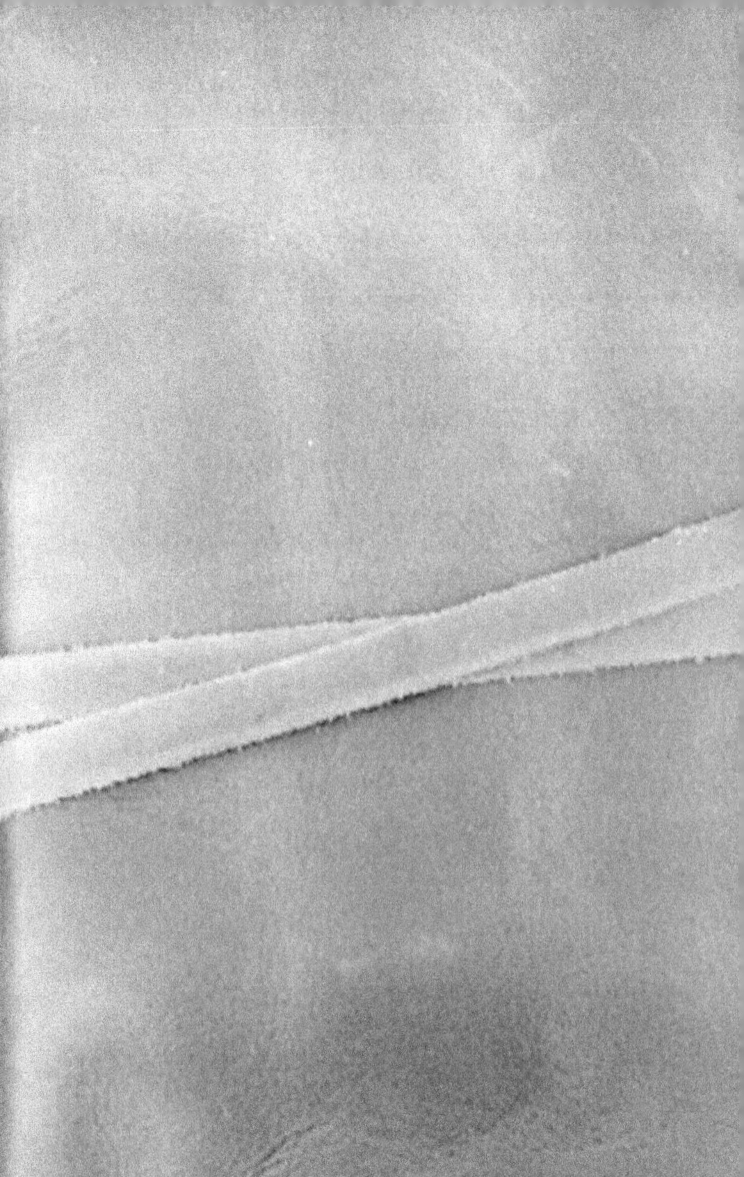

The Execution of Plans

Kane finished penning the words in his journal entry about Zuan's machine. Wondering whether he had made the right decision, he closed the book and took a minute to contemplate his life captured within the pages. The tome was more than history; it was *his story.*

In the days following the time Kane spent with Zuan and the machine, Abaddon had captured Zuan, and today was execution day. If Kane was to make it to the evening event on time, then he needed to leave now.

Kane hid the diary in its usual spot behind the hand-carved chest he had made over a century ago. As he reached for his knapsack resting on the lid, he shivered with the uncomfortable feeling of being watched. A new urgency filled his chest and caused him to move even more quickly for the door. He paused only a second to take a quick glance over his shoulder. His humble abode would be rudimentary in most eyes, but to him, it was all he needed. He had spent a number of years here, so perhaps it was time to find a new place. He resolved to change his location after today. Given Abaddon's plans for Zuan, it was probably for the best.

Kane passed right by the cloaked Gabor as he hurried off to witness the "surprise celebration" that Abaddon had been advertising to the dwellers.

The trek to the event took all day and afforded Kane some time to think. He wondered whether Abaddon would actually go through with it, and whether Sook would intercede on his son's behalf. And then there was the question of the sealed ones. What would happen to them?

Before he could finalize his planned responses (and possible escapes) to the many potential outcomes for the day, Kane arrived on the scene. It was obvious that Abaddon had spared no expense in preparation for the main event and the accompanying festivities. The decorations and revelry far surpassed even the best-celebrated holidays.

Abaddon, in all his pomp, made his grand entrance. Half his crew heralded his entry with song and dance, and the other half marched behind in formal military cadence (no doubt, in case Sook showed up).

After a brief speech from Abaddon claiming that Zuan had been lying about his identity to scam the dwellers, he instructed some instigators to open the curtains on the platform to reveal a beaten Zuan attached to an execution post. Sickness in Kane's gut wrestled with that growing in his heart. The bloody Zuan was virtually unrecognizable, save for his eyes.

Some of the crowd cheered and others protested. Several of the watchers and instigators were hedging bets over the spoils of the event. Kane fell to his knees in anguish as Abaddon started the one-minute countdown for the execution.

Zuan raised his head and looked in Kane's direction. His green eyes penetrated through the crowd and found Kane's. They burned with hope and life, showing no fear. Kane instantly knew that all would be okay. He was convinced that Sook must be on the way to rescue his son. As the crowd counted down the seconds for the vile act, Kane counted them for Sook's arrival.

"Ten..."

This can't really be happening, can it?

"Nine..."

Surely Sook will come.

"Eight...seven...six...five...four...three..."

Any second now. Kane fought the urge to shield his eyes from the pending atrocity.

"Two!"

"ONE!"

The fatal blow ensued.
Both life and plan were executed.

Beam Me Up

Not even seconds after Zuan's death, his body mysteriously disappeared. Most didn't notice at first because they were still reeling from the horror. However, the vanishing act didn't escape Abaddon's notice. His face was terror-stricken. His followers started falling to their knees and waving their hands in the air to concede their ignorance and evade Abaddon's wrath.

Both dwellers and visitors commenced a frantic search for Zuan's body. They turned over every stone, including pebbles, as if a dead body could hide under one.

The chaos and confusion intensified when various dwellers spontaneously started to glow. Their faces shone like torches in the night. It was the seal—Sook's seal—from the machine.

Kane felt the emerging sting across his face, too. It felt like an invisible finger of fire igniting a word across his forehead. Yes, he had chosen the machine. He had chosen renewal.

A calm fell over the crowd as the sky lit up with a brilliant light. It seemed bright enough to hurt the eyes (much brighter than either of the two suns); however, it produced no pain. Once the light peaked in intensity, the dwellers with the seal began to lift off the ground and float upward. Sook was beaming his dwellers up. He had come for them as promised.

Kane felt his feet release the ground. The light beam seemed to pull at the inside of him. His celestial energy was being ripped from his planetarium form. He momentarily shifted his gaze toward his physical body, which began to disintegrate and fall to the ground like shredded paper. It was as if his being was celebrating the moment and showering the ones left behind with confetti. The dematerialization of his head induced faintness. He embraced the ensuing freedom and submitted to the loss of consciousness.

The Zenith

After what seemed like the briefest of moments, Kane awakened to find himself standing before the throne of Sook. All memory of the events between the floating experience and the throne room was irretrievable.

The all-white room was bathed in reverence. Kane, unsure whether to speak, bow, or cry, tried to take it all in without moving a muscle. He eventually inched his eyes toward the throne, yet still was not able to look directly at Sook.

Sook broke the stillness with his thunderous voice. "Bring me the book written of Kane."

Kane could feel Sook's eyes upon him now. It was as if his gaze displaced everything around him. The deafening silence and the weight of Sook's look were almost unbearable.

Out of the corner of his eye, Kane saw Gabor the courier enter the chamber carrying a book, and he breathed in relief. The reprieve quickly dissipated, however, when he noticed that the book was his own personal journal from behind the wooden chest.

Gabor handed the book to Sook, causing Kane to fall to his knees. Kane knew the contents of the journal and how most of it blasphemed Sook. He cringed at the idea of Sook reading his inner thoughts about him. Had he written his own demise? Everything that he had done or thought—good or bad—was written in that book. But not yet recorded in the book was how he had let all that hatred go with the help of Zuan and his machine. How could he ever convince Sook that the writer of the book was not same being now standing before his throne?

Out of Kane gushed apologies, excuses, and confessions. Sook raised his hand as an indication for Kane to cease. Once again, the solemn silence beat his ears and he hopelessly dropped his head in defeat.

Zuan spoke up. (Although unnoticed by Kane until now, he had been standing beside him the entire time.)

"I hereby request a full pardon for Kane and his transgressions against you, Commander Sook, against himself, and against all others in his life," said Zuan.

Sook slowly nodded his head in agreement to the appeal. Unsure of what had just happened, Kane began to weep with tears of gratitude over the grace bestowed upon him.

After more uncomfortable silence, Sook finally addressed Kane. "You are forgiven and your transgressions are forever forgotten." His words were firm, yet laced with a loving mercy.

"I planted each dweller on Ge," Sook continued, "for a purpose. And your purpose was to be an important advisor in my kingdom. I specifically gave you gifts of observation and reporting so that you could help me stay informed. However, you chose to turn your allegiance to Abaddon and work for him.

"Because I will reap what I sow, and because I can take the bad and turn it into good, I still used your service to Abaddon to meet my needs. I didn't have to assign a separate observer to spy on Abaddon—we just needed to follow you, his most used watcher.

"You gave away Abaddon's plans by the dwellers you watched. The information you recorded in your journal was like a report for our side. For example, you reported to Abaddon about Zuan, which prompted him to plan the execution. The extravagant event ensured that Abaddon and all his top officials would be congregated at a site away from his kingdom. Because of what you wrote in the journal, we knew where Abaddon hid the keys to his energy furnace, and Zuan was able to retrieve them right after the execution released him from his terrestrial suit, thus rendering him able to move about unhindered. All of this thanks to the purpose you fulfilled, whether you intended it for my benefit or not."

When Sook finished his explanation, he allowed Kane a few moments to digest it all before continuing.

"Kane, *you* have been renewed, redeemed, and now reconciled to me. You will now join Zuan in my next endeavor."

Kane was beside himself at the opportunity for a second chance.

All Things Renewed

As the multitude led by Zuan entered Planet Ge's atmosphere, it no doubt looked to the remaining inhabitants like the sky was splitting and the stars were falling. This fast-approaching force all shared the same energy as Sook, and so they were in like mind and one accord. They were coming for the final battle.

At Zuan's side, Kane was not returning as a dirty dweller or as a cursed creature, but as a renewed being with a renewed purpose. Now he understood the bigger picture after Zuan had explained everything before leaving Sook's. Zuan told him about how, long before the dwellers existed, Sook had seen a change in Abaddon that would eventually lead to his defection. Even before anything had begun to manifest, Sook had already been making plans. His intentions were to move his capital to Ge, where he would have eternal followers who would never fall away like Abaddon and his cohorts.

Sook purposely left Abaddon to rule on Ge and thus create a divide between the dwellers, so that Sook could weed out the bad ones and harvest the good ones. Now Abaddon's lease on authority was up; Sook was reclaiming Ge and bringing his kingdom capital there.

Kane snapped from his thoughts when the convoy landed on Ge. There before them stood Abaddon and his army. Kane couldn't remember Abaddon looking so dark. His energy had obviously transformed, giving him a solid black appearance—so much so, that when his arm passed in front of his body, it was imperceivable. A stark contrast to Zuan, who was dressed in royal garb and bathed in pure white energy.

Being the good commander that he is, Sook permits everyone one last chance at redemption—including Abaddon, who was afforded lots of time on Ge to reconsider his decision. Today was reckoning day and time was up. Zuan had offered Abaddon the same choice for renewal and restoration, but he had declined it, unlike Kane.

Abaddon's refusal was the first act of war in the great final battle. Both forces fought with fervor, yet only Sook's army possessed the power to win. Abaddon was soon placed in chains and deposited in his own furnace to burn for eternity with his followers.

Once Ge was secured, an enormous light consumed the sky. This time it was Sook, bringing his entire city. He would rule from Ge with his inextinguishable followers forever.

Kane realized that his previous life on Ge was a mere refining effort—a process of energy renewal. Now he was truly alive. All things renewed.

Review Request

I hope you have enjoyed this short story about second chances and personal renewal. If so, then please let other readers know. Let's share the knowledge and help people to find the Great Renewer of us all.

About the Author

BEYR REYES received her doctorate degree in biomedical science. She has produced over 200 publications in science, medicine, and Christian genres.

You can contact Beyr Reyes via email, Twitter, or Facebook (Beyr is Jennifer Minigh's pen name):

Beyr.Reyes@ShadeTreePublishing.com

@JenniferMinigh

Facebook.com/Jennifer.Minigh

Other Books
by Beyr Reyes

489: a short story about forgiveness

2016 CSPA general fiction book of the year

Loaded with plot twists and surprises, this short story delivers a powerful message about forgiveness and how our lives affect other people, even those we don't know. Widely endorsed by therapists, this book helps readers to be set free from the bondage of unforgiveness.

Make a Choice

2011 Readers' Favorite Silver Award

This book is a continuum of revelation designed to challenge your foundational beliefs and then challenge you to stand on those beliefs. In Unit 1 (Choose Your Beliefs), you will ask yourself questions like: Is God really God? Is Jesus God? Is the Bible true? In Unit 2 (Live Like You Mean It), you will ask yourself: Am I really a Christian? Am I really saved? Am I really forgiven? All along the way, you will make decisions that will affect your life forever.

Fast Answers:
When You Need Answers Now

Other fasting books tell you why to fast or explain the importance thereof, but leave you guessing how to even start. This book puts legs on your intentions so that you can walk it out. *Fast Answers* has mapped out fasting plans with a clear starting point, destination, and goal. The plans come in one-, three-, or seven-day varieties and are tailored to specific prayer needs. No longer will you fumble your way through a fast. With this book, you will find your way to the answers you need right now. This book isn't about fast answers (as in quick ones). It's about fast answers (as in seeking-God ones).

Subject Your Flesh

2014 CSPA e-book of the year

Need to get control of your life? Tired of constant dieting? Fed up with bad habits? Subjection is the answer that lasts. Learn how to eradicate the problem areas in your life. Take control of your flesh and turn your life around using the Word of God.

The Big Picture
2011 Readers' Favorite Bronze Award

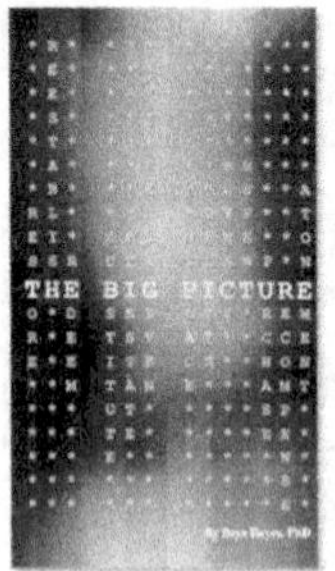

Most folks know the stories about Creation, the Jewish nation, and Jesus, but they don't know how all these things are connected. This book provides a broad perspective of the Bible that will help the beginner place events and their purposes together. For the readers who always have their heads buried in certain passages, this book is a refreshing step back to help illuminate the big picture.

Your Write Calling:
Is Writing Right for You?

Have you been toying with the idea of becoming a writer? If so, this book is for you. Learn what it means, and what it takes, to be a Christian writer. After reading this book, you will understand what the call to write looks like. In addition, you will know how to get equipped and what to write. Endorsed by Jerry B. Jenkins, this book contains soul-searching questions to help you decide on your calling all along the way.